What Tough Times Taught Me . . . .

that I just gotta teach you

In the Spirit of Greatness,

Meagha Soland

What Tough Times Taught Me . . .

that I just gotta teach you

MORALS & VALUES PRESS
A Division of Greatness Now!

ISBN 0-9754191-5-3

Printed in the United States of America

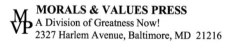 **MORALS & VALUES PRESS**
A Division of Greatness Now!
2327 Harlem Avenue, Baltimore, MD 21216

*For every time I thought to give up
yet made the choice to stay the course—
to God be the glory.*

ACKNOWLEDGEMENTS

There are a host of persons who were instrumental in me making it to the other side of what I contend was one of the most devastating periods of my life.

First and foremost, I honor and praise My God, the keeper of my mind. Grateful am I for how He never ever fails to hold me up, especially during the days when I thought about giving up.

Second, I would like to extend my appreciation to my biological sisters, Tamiel and Jodi for allowing me and James to stay at their homes when we were initially displaced and for the many other ways you both showed your support.

Third, I would like to extend my appreciation to Regina, Aunt Bettye, Deloris, Lisa and Andre for opening up their home to me and for making me feel comfortable when I had to stay over for a night or two or three.

Fourth, I would like to extend my appreciation to Maurice for the use of your car whenever I needed it; to Carlos for picking me up and dropping me off at the office; to Sharon (the best mentor mom in the world) for unwavering moral support; to Kumasi, Jamaal, Angela, Alex, Omi, Jackie, Bernice, Elizabeth, Annette, Dr. McPhatter, and Joan for the money, the gift cards, groceries, furniture, prayers, emails and greeting cards with encouraging words. You all will never understand how your being there blessed me and gave me the strength to face each day with that much more determination.

Finally, to my sons who have always made hanging in there worth doing. You both, in your own unique way, have always caused me to stand even in my weakest of moments. Love you!

CONTENTS

Why I Had to Write this Book

On a good day, I am a lively, fun, peaceful, intelligent, ambitious, determined, confident, very articulate, incredibly gifted, and quite an attractive woman of African Descent. I love life. I am tickled pink in love with myself. I am proud of my accomplishments. I treasure with my whole heart my God and the relationship we have. I know what I have been called to do, and I wake up every morning more committed than the day before to operate in the calling that has been placed upon my life.

All of this withstanding, not one of these factors prevented the bottom from dropping out of my world during what I felt was the toughest season of my life thus far. In no way did I see the devastation coming, and by no account did I feel that what I was going through was warranted. Yet, right before my very eyes unbelievable things were happening that I could not control. My life as I knew it was severely out of control and it did not seem like God was the least bit moved by all that was going on at all.

Could it be that He was not moved because He was upset with me? Could it be that this was pay back for the times I did not do what He told me to do or say what He told me to say? Had God in fact given the enemy permission to wreak havoc in my life as He did Job? Or was my own wrongdoing, bad choices, and irresponsible decisions coming back to haunt me?

Whatever be the case, I was made to come to the hard, fast conclusion that no matter how "good" we are. No matter how cultivated or refined we are. No matter how handsome, cute, sexy, or beautiful we think we are. No matter how much we love God. No matter how much we believe God loves us. No matter how anointed, prophetic, or great we profess to be. No matter where we live, what we drive, or how much money we make, life is going to come unraveled. We are going to hurt deeply. And we are going to find ourselves completely confounded and utterly shocked by the audacity of something or someone. Like it or not. Prepared or not.

I was abruptly ushered into this most profound reality on September of 2005, when the real estate broker who was supposed to help save me home and put me in a position of being debt free, ended up causing me to lose my home by breaching a contract we had entered into.

The breach of contract was devastating on so many levels as it resulted in me having to enter into a long court battle to hold this fraudulent man accountable. It resulted in me having to break the news to my sons that we had to move out of the home I had owned for six years and we had come to know as our peaceful refuge after my divorce. But more importantly, the breach of contract resulted in all of us not having a place to call home.

To this day, I don't know which was more painful; being betrayed and then ignored by a man whom I trusted with something as valuable as my living quarters. Receiving the news that I had loss the court battle to stay in my home. Or February 28, 2006, when I stood in the living room of my empty house crying profusely because for the first time in thirty eight years of living I was about to be displaced...and could not do a damn thing about it.

If these dynamics weren't bad enough, the chain of events that subsequently followed the loss of my home just about sucked the very life out of me. If I wasn't crying and feeling helpless because my youngest son and I were no longer residing under the same roof, then I was crying and feeling betrayed because a huge consulting contract that I had was pulled right from under my nose—without so much as an explanation. If I wasn't crying and feeling confused because of the failure of the national conference that I and others had invested so much time, energy, and finances in, then I was crying and feeling lost because for three months the nights fell upon the days and with each night I found myself not knowing where I would lay my head next.

Torture is what it felt like to have so much going so wrong in such a short period of time. In my field of work, I had served a many people who found themselves in my situation. I had guided a many people in the direction of resources that could potentially turn their situation around. But never did I think, not for one minute, that I would find myself in the same position of those I had once served. Not that I ever thought I was any better than those I served. It's just that I guess I always wanted to believe that being armed with the right information serves as somewhat of a buffer or even a barrier to one falling on life-shattering hard times.

Unfortunately, some of us – smart though we think we are – are ignorantly under the impression that if we live right. (Whatever that means . . . .) If we treat people right. If we go to church. If we pray regularly, being mindful to repent from our ungodly ways of old. If we take care of our children. If we mind our business and leave other folks' business alone. Or, if we seek to sincerely do God's will for our lives, we will find ourselves exempt from life's strong arm. This, I'm afraid, is just not so.

To the contrary, you can read your spiritual text everyday. You can love those who despitefully use you. You can preach, pray and prophesy. You can feed the hungry, clothe the naked, and provide shelter to the homeless. You can refrain from speaking evil of anyone. You can give God the first of your earnings. You can make the wisest decisions, yet you can still find yourself, as I did, despondently looking to the hills from whence cometh your help, asking, *"Lord, where art thou?"*

Having said that, I wrote this book because as I found myself safely, *safely, safely, safely* on the other side of the most difficult season of my life, (after taking several deep, deep breaths) there was an urging in my spirit to reach back and help lighten the blow for someone who may be as dumbfounded as I found myself when the storm came. I wrote this book to help ease the pain for someone who is working ever so feverishly to put the pieces of them self back together, yet keeps getting in their own way. And I wrote this book to validate the thoughts of that someone who has more questions than they will ever get answers to.

To you I say, instead of trying to undue what has already been done. Instead of attempting to control what you cannot control. Or instead of continuing to ignore what is undoubtedly right in your face, focus your attention on getting from where you are to where you would like to be. Focus your energy on making certain that all of your decisions are strategically aligned with the route of your destination, and by all means employ God's strength to be made perfect in your time(s) of weakness.

Believe me when I tell you that being restored from tough times is not a cake walk. Neither is it something to take lightly. The restoration process is like that of most processes; it takes work. It takes time. And it takes a made up mind. In fact, I would venture to say that the more made up one's mind is and the more committed one is to the work of being restored, the quicker restoration occurs.

I began writing this book in April of 2007, which was a little less than a year from the time the bottom dropped out of my little world. At the time of penning, everything that I lost...I mean everything that I lost had been restored unto me, and not just restored but restored beyond anything that I could ask, think or imagine. Amazingly enough, God has positioned me in such a way that if I did not tell someone what I went through no one would ever know. To the average on-looker it appeared and still appears that Mischa has never missed a beat; which in and of itself is nothing more than the favor of God reigning in my life.

Although I tried to, and to some extent wanted to keep *my story* to *myself* God just was not having it. He was determined that my experience would serve to bless, encourage, and inspire someone else as they hoped against hope…attempting to internalize the truth that while tough times don't last forever tough people absolutely do.

My prayer is that you be strengthened in your faith as you share in the lessons I learned while going through what represented tough times for me. Surprisingly, among the many things I was fortunate to learn, I truly learned what Mischa is made of. And today I proudly report that this here woman is made of some really, really rich stuff.

Mischa

What Tough Times Taught Me . . .
that I just gotta teach you

CHAPTER ONE

You Must Have Something to Hold On To

"An anchored soul can't drift but so far."

Like a small boat making its was across a sea that has been hit with unforeseen tumultuous winds, tough times can toss one to and fro causing one to experience a sudden yet sure loss of control over an otherwise controlled situation.

One minute the waters are calm and peaceful, just the way you imagined they would be as you stepped on the boat to set sail. The scenery around you is both relaxing and breathtaking just as you anticipated it would be. Then, out of nowhere what was once calm and controlled is now chaotic and costing. What was once relaxing and breathtaking is now tense and awkward.

But what in the world happened? Where did the craziness, chaos, and confusion come from? How is one supposed to stop or gain control over something that seems so uncontrollable? Who will come and provide a sense of solace and stability to a situation that is quickly getting more and more out of control? Why did this have to happen now, at a time when preparedness is not even a part of the equation? What happened to a warning...? Perhaps just a little warning may have been helpful.

These are just some of the questions we ask ourselves when we are confronted with the raging winds of tough times; questions we mentally work to get answers to when life shows up without notice and without us extending an invitation to life to wreak havoc on our psyches.

Why the analogy of the boat, the calm waters, the beautiful scenery coming face-to-face with tumultuous winds, and a shifting sea? Well, this is the best way to describe what occurred in my life from September 2005 to August 2006.

As I shared in the "Why I Had to Write This Book" section, I never ever thought that I would experience life so out of control. I would have never predicted that in my lifetime I would see myself in such a rock bottom state where nothing...I mean nothing seemed to be going in my favor. Where literally every time I turned around a new storm was on the horizon. Every time I turned around the winds of tribulation were becoming that much more unbearable, and just about everything that I thought was a guarantee had become a negotiable.

One loss after another loss after another loss is what my reality turned in to. In my mind I kept asking, "Is there any rest for the weary?" I kept asking, "Is it really true that God won't put anymore on you than you can bear? And does He really know how much I can bear?" I kept asking, "Is God perhaps mistaking Mischa's strength for someone else's strength?" Because for real, the Mischa I know; the Mischa I've lived with for the past thirty nine years is not equipped for this kind of pressure and uncertainty. And if God knows me like He says He does, He too knows this as well.

Well, as things changed and changed and changed what I quickly realized was that crying and questioning God was not going to make accepting what *was* any more bearable. Rather, I concluded that I had to find something that I knew I could grab a hold to; something with sustaining power; something I could anchor myself in as I weathered this very unsuspecting, unpredictable, and seemingly unceasing stormy season. In fact, this something is what I said I could and would dare to believe in as my situation became increasingly unbelievable.

For me this something ended up being my faith. My faith in God. My faith in a never failing, all knowing, never changing, able, loving God that ultimately and astoundingly kept me as I endured through.

For others *it* may be something else. Why, because every individual is different. Additionally, where you are with respect to your mindset and your growth determines to a great degree what your *it* is. Let's face it, some are kept by drugs. Some are kept by alcohol. Some are kept by shopping. Some are kept by relationships—unhealthy and destructive though they may be. Some are kept by food; yet others are kept by habitually participating in meaningless acts of sex with partners who have absolutely nothing at all to offer besides the sex itself.

Although, on my worst days, I thought about turning to one or two of the things I mentioned above, my mind quickly put me in touch with the times before when I had chosen (out of desperation and immaturity) sex or shopping or relationships as a means by which to help me cope with what I couldn't change as well as the results those choices yielded. Upon having these series of flashbacks I decided that I wasn't willing to put myself in such a compromising position again.

I had come too far in my growth and development, and despite how painful my right now situation was, I knew that I could not afford to chance adding any more drama to my life by consciously making irresponsible decisions. I just wasn't going to do it.

So what did I do? I anchored myself...and when I say anchored myself, I mean I anchored myself in my faith with a determination and a commitment that come hell or high water I was going to take my last breath – if it came down to that – trusting God. From the time I opened my eyes in the morning, to several times a day, to before I closed my eyes at night, I was mindful to tell God how much I trusted Him. I told Him how much I loved Him. I told Him how much I believed in Him. I told Him that I believed He could and was in fact working to change my situation. However, (as difficult as it was) I also told Him that if my situation never changed. If I continued to lose and never gained another thing, He was still my God and in Him I would continue to trust.

Some days, with tears streaming down my face to the point that I couldn't see anything in front of me; or crying to a point where my head felt like it was about to explode, I declared my love, appreciation, and admiration for the God who had brought me so far. Some days when I felt so heavy that I could not form words, I wrote to Him about how grateful I was that things were as well as they were.

Things didn't look good. Things didn't feel good. And in some respects they weren't good. Yet my experiences with God through the course of many, many years let me know that He is GOOD, and if I could simply muster up enough faith and strength and belief in just how good He is—I would in fact be alright.

And guess what? I am alright! Today, I am alright! I am, today, an even greater force to reckon with. I am, today, stronger in my faith than I have ever been before. Now, was it easy to look at my situation and still believe? No. Was it easy to consistently proclaim love for a God that I knew could change my situation overnight, yet chose to change it over time? No, it was not. Not in the least bit.

Through it all, what I am most grateful for however are the things I learned as a result of choosing to trust God; as a result of choosing to believe in God; as a result of choosing to love Him for who He is and not for what He does. Today, I am convinced and fully persuaded that the sweetest place of our spiritual journey is where God being God is predicated on His power rather than on His promises.

What do I mean? What I mean is simply this, if you live long enough, and if you experience enough life in your living, you will reach a place where what you have read in your spiritual text (His promises) will not hold as much weight as what you have actually seen God do right before your very eyes (His power), be it in your life or in someone else's life.

It is in this place – believe it or not – that your faith is being solidified. It is in and through seasons such as these (the tough times) that who God is in your life changes, and changes drastically. And the reason for the change is as you go through...as we go through – providing we go through in the right spirit – what God is essentially doing is taking us through an elevation process.

He's getting some stuff out of us, and at the same time He's depositing some stuff in us. He's purging us, and at the same time He's preparing us. He's breaking us down, and at the same time He's building us up. He's shaking your spiritual foundation, and at the same time He's re-setting your spiritual foundation. He's removing some people, and at the same time He's drawing you closer to Him. Thus we undoubtedly lose some things. And in some cases, we may lose *every thing*. But what we lose can never ever compare to what we ultimately gain. Never.

CHAPTER TWO

You Must Be Surrounded by Strong People

"Strength is more than relative, it's relevant."

Somewhere inside of myself I have always understood that there is truth in the correlation between the company we keep, their influence upon us, and how their influence ultimately influences our decisions as well as our behavior. At the same time, however, I thought that I was slick enough, smart enough, and even spiritual enough that this principle, if you will, did not apply to Mischa.

As a teenager, I really thought that I could hang around negative or stagnate people and still be positive and progressive. As a young adult, I thought that what others were not doing with their lives would have no impact at all upon what I essentially did with my life. As a grown woman, I figured, if those around me wanted to sell themselves short by accepting more lies than truth; if they chose to just dwell on what wasn't going right in their lives; if they just wanted to go day in and day out simply existing but not living in the fullness of what God had purposed for their lives, well that was their decision and it had no bearing on me.

Well, not so. And it wasn't until I had to endure one of the toughest seasons of my life that I came to terms with just how *not so* this really is. As the days became more difficult; as the tears became more frequent; as it became more apparent that there was the possibility that I would be in the uncomfortable place I was in for a while longer than I initially had hoped, who I talked to, what I talked with them about, and how often I talked to them became critical.

It was no longer about just having friends. It was no longer about just having associates...people I simply knew. Neither was it about how many degrees my friends had, how many zeros where in their salary, how big their house was, or what model car they drove. I needed to know that you believed. I needed to know that you had a conviction(s) that you held fast to. I needed to know that you wanted something out of life, and was willing to do whatever it took to get where you desired to be.

Why were these things important? Well, they were important because if you don't have sense enough to want something great for yourself; if you don't possess the presence of mind to call on a power greater than you in the time of trouble; if you don't have the type of truth abiding in you that has the ability to render one free from lies, and depression, and low self esteem, and bondage on whatever level, you would not be able to speak life to me as I fought my way through my season of uncertainty.

When I finally found out that I had been taken and had in fact loss my home to an unethical real estate broker, I didn't need to pick up the phone and call someone who would be on the other end saying, "Girl, that's a shame. You got every reason in the world to feel like throwing in the towel." Or, "Girl, you just can't trust those real estate people. That's why I never bought a house and probably won't ever buy a house." Or, "Mischa, I hear about so many real estate scams it ain't funny. Just sue his pants off, teach him a lesson, and maybe he'll think twice about doing this to somebody else."

No. I needed to hear affirming, empowering, live-giving words like, "Though you may feel violated and taken advantage of, the same God who blessed you to purchase that house will bless you to purchase another house." Or, "Girl, don't spend another day wallowing in why it happened, pick yourself up, and be about the business of doing what you need to do to move yourself and your boys forward." Or, "Mischa, I realize that your loss has been substantial yet it is nothing to be compared to what has to be on the other side of this."

Words like these coming from the mouths of people who are not just about speaking to have something to say, rather are governed themselves by words that truly define how they live their lives is what helped to make the difference in how I was able to keep believing that losing my house was not the worse thing that could've happened to me. My friends, and even some associates came through for me in such a huge way where their faith was concerned. Folk that I had never spent any time talking faith with spoke faith to my wounded spirit in such a way that I was compelled to hold on.

Time and time again, in particular those days when I was at my lowest, it seemed to never fail that the phone would ring, or a card would arrive, or an e-mail would come to remind me I was not in this thing alone. At the same time, slowly but surely those persons who had been in my life that didn't possess any positivism, real strength, or faith were weeded out—one way or another. Either I found that I stopped calling them because of the limitedness of what they had to say. Or they stopped calling me because of what they didn't know to say.

Things for me had become a matter of life or death. I could not afford to play around with my survival. I could not afford to fake it. I had to know what I knew. I had to live what I knew. And I had to be strategically surrounded by those who knew what I didn't; those who were grounded enough in their faith that I could borrow from their faith while mine was yet being restored.

When I tell you that my circle got smaller and smaller as the days, weeks, and months went by, I mean just that. Some friendships were reduced to acquaintanceships. Some acquaintanceships were elevated to friendships. Some family members were moved from the front row of my life to the balcony. While others were put out of the theater all together; no longer privileged to witness the grand production entitled *"The Life of Mischa Green: A Woman in Pursuit of Everything God Has for Her."* And I was, after a brief period of struggle, okay with all of the shifts and changes. I had to be, particularly when I came to the realization that the changes were indeed in my best interest.

During the course of this purging process I *eventually* yielded and gave God permission (if there is such a thing) to search every aspect of my life and remove that which He felt would not serve me well as He ushered me into a new realm of faith. I became so desperate to be everything He designed me to be that I did not care what it was – person, place, or thing – that He had to eliminate. I just knew that life for me had to be different and was going to be different. I knew that life for me was going to be richer and more purposeful.

I further knew that not everybody was going to be able to handle where God was taking me and what He was doing in my life. Not everybody was going to be receptive. Not everybody would be able to celebrate my elevation. Why, because everybody is not ready for everything, which essentially translated to me, *"Mischa, some folk aren't going with you from here. This is in fact the last stop with him, her, and them in tow. So say your good-byes, let them folk off, and keep the train moving."*

Difficult though it may have been in some instances, I did just that. And the good news is I have been the better for it! I now have the benefit of knowing that those I am blessed to have in my inner circle are in it to win it—for me as well as for themselves. They believe in their own success. They believe in my success. And whatever we have to do to ensure that success is ours that is simply what we have to do. Plain and simple.

CHAPTER THREE

You Must Have a Survival Language

"The beauty of words is not the words.
The beauty of words is the power emanating from
the person speaking the words."

I can't. I don't feel like it. I don't want to. It doesn't take
all of that. Enough is enough. I don't have no more
strength. I can't take anymore bad news. If another thing
happens I am just going to lose my mind. I see why
people give up and stop trying. What kind of God would
let so much devastation happen to one person? Please, I
don't care what you say, there can't be a God. I thought
bad things didn't happen to good people. Shucks, my life
was a lot simpler before I started getting into this spiritual

stuff. It was so much easier to do things my way than it is to keep trying to do the "right" thing.

For too many of us it comes down to this type of verbiage when we feel betrayed by life, by God, by those we love, and those we thought loved us. All it takes, in many instances, is for too much to happen too quick and go on for too long before we start singing a new song. The hope we used to have, we don't have anymore. The survival skills we once clung to somehow get away from us, and the result ends up being a defeatist mentality.

Where some of us may have been very positive, optimistic thinkers that never allowed the pressures of life to get the best of us; where others of us may be very pro-active doers who pride ourselves on being five to ten steps ahead of the game thus always prepared for the inevitably, living long enough, as I have learned, will have the most optimistic among us imprisoned by circumstances that are so profound they rob us of our courage, of our fortitude, of our dignity, yea even of our survival language—whether for the short term or the long term.

It took a couple of months of tough times and a good friend for me to realize that I had in fact become a victim of what I just described. I shall never forget the conversation. I had spent the past four or so nights in my office sleeping on the sofa, living out of a duffle bag when the reality of my situation brought me to a place of crying uncontrollably. I just could not take the isolation another day. I did not want to stay in that office on that sofa another night by myself. I did not want to wash up in the public bathroom one more morning with the anxiety that someone would knock on the door needing to use the facilities as I cleaned myself up in the only place that was available to me.

I needed company. I needed to sleep in a bed. I needed to bathe in a tub. I needed to feel normal. I also needed to share my needs with someone that I could trust; someone that would not judge me. Ultimately, though, I needed to share my needs with someone who had the ability and would not think twice about helping me. Someone who would open their home and allow me the good night's sleep my soul craved so desperately for. It was in this moment I reluctantly picked up the phone and reached out to my girlfriend Lisa.

Initially I called Lisa's cell phone. She didn't answer. I then called Lisa's home phone. Again, she didn't answer.

I hung up more devastated than I was before I called. Why, because before my rock bottom experience I did not believe in asking for help, therefore, I had to muster up everything that I could to make the call in the first place. I could not believe that there was no answer. Immediately I began to cry and go into my victim mode. *"Why wasn't Lisa answering? I knew that she was who the Lord told me to call. I was clear...I knew that I couldn't just call anybody, so I prayed. I asked God to direct me. I specifically asked Him to tell me who I could get help from...right now, and Lisa was the name I heard. I know it. So where was she? Why wasn't she answering her phones? Why, Lord? You told me to call her. Now where is she? Where is Lisa, Lord?"* This is the monologue that I had with myself—while crying like I had just been told the worse news of my life.

A few hours or so after hanging up from my second attempt to reach Lisa, she called me back. As I talked with her I shared my situation; a situation that until then Lisa knew not the extent of. Although she knew about the loss of my house, she did not know that things had come down to me staying in the office and sleeping on the sofa. I was scared. I was perplexed, yet I knew that relief was in becoming vulnerable. And so I told her. Through my tears I told her everything. From where I had been sleeping, to where I had been bathing, to how I just couldn't take one more night of it. I said that I desperately needed company; that I desperately needed to sleep in a warm, comfortable bed; and that I desperately needed some peace of mind.

Get this: Believe it or not, Lisa and her mom were one hour . . . just one hour from leaving town to go away for four days when I left the voice mail messages on Lisa's home and cell phones. As Lisa and I spoke, with the compassion that Lisa always embodies, she said, *"Sha, I'm so sorry. I didn't know."* She said, *"Me and mommy are preparing to leave town in about an hour. Give me a minute, let me see if I can maneuver some things, and I will call you right back."* She told me to stop crying. She told me that everything was going to be alright. She reminded me that God had not left me in spite of how it felt.

I told Lisa that in my heart-of-hearts I knew that God had not gone anywhere, but I was tired. I was just tired of going through. I was tired of fighting to hold on. I was tired of wishing for something to change. I told her that I didn't know how much longer I could hold on.

An hour had gone by and Lisa had not called me back. I then started going up in my head thinking that she had perhaps forgotten about me. I thought that maybe she couldn't do the maneuvering that she thought she could, and just didn't know how to tell me. Then I said to myself, *"Mischa, instead of sitting her crying and wondering, why not just pick up the phone and call Lisa back. So what she might think you're being inpatient. So what she might think that you're trying to pressure her. You need help NOW!"*

Some years ago I attended a Women's Bible Study Series at New Psalmist Baptist Church where Dr. Carolyn Showell was the guest preacher. And she said, *"Desperate people do desperate things."* There was no question about how desperate I was, and in my desperate place I could not chance Lisa forgetting about me. Not that I thought she would. Again, I just wasn't willing to take the chance. So I called back.

When I called Lisa back she said that she was just about to call me. In response to my initial request, she said, *"Sha, I don't usually do this, but because of who you are and what you mean to me I am going to offer you my home as a place to rest for the next four days while I'm gone."* She said, *"Come here, regain your strength, and strategize a plan for what your next steps will be. But most of all I want you to find some peace while you're here."* She further said, *"Sha, we serve a faithful God and I am believing that He will make things better for you soon."*

After I hung up from speaking with Lisa, while I was waiting for her to bring me the keys to her house, I began to think and think and think. I thought about my situation, and the fact that I had actually called her to stay at her place because I was in fact *homeless*. I kept repeating *homeless...homeless...homeless.* Then I asked myself what I had been doing or not doing to rectify my current lot.

Well, as I talked with myself, and as I reflected upon the conversation that I had with Lisa I realized that more often than not I kept using the words *I can't* or *I don't want to* or *it's not getting any better*; those disempowering words that have no redemptive value or restorative properties at all. It was then that I also realized that amidst the chaos and mayhem I had surrendered my survival language; which greatly contributed to why things stayed the same. Because whether you know it or not, ninety percent of surviving – regardless of what we are working to survive through – is in how we think; what we tell ourselves.

How we think subsequently influences both what we say and how we behave.

To know me is to know that I have the capacity to help the most discouraged person find encouragement. In fact, my father in ministry once told me that I possessed the gift of encouragement. Yet the tougher times got the more difficult it was for me to speak those things that are not as though they were. The tougher times got the quicker I forgot that as a man thinketh so is he/she. Without even noticing, *I can* was replaced with *I can't*. *God will* was replaced with *God might*. I said that I wasn't a victim, yet I found myself acting like a victim and speaking like a victim.

However, during those four days at Lisa's house I replenished my survival language arsenal. I looked myself in the mirror and recommitted myself and my tongue to only speaking life to my situation. I challenged myself to think about the counsel I would give to someone else in my situation. How would I encourage them? What would I tell them to say to themselves despite how bleak or dismal things looked? These were in fact the same things I had to declare upon my own life everyday...all day. Regardless of how bad things appeared I had to stand my ground, choose my words wisely, and walk in the power of my words as a demonstration of how earnestly I believed what I was telling myself.

It was not two weeks later...two weeks later I tell you that my situation began to turn around. By the power of my own conviction, deliverance came. By the power of my own proclamation, hope was restored. Why? Because it is one thing to surround oneself with those who know what to say, however, it is something all together different to allow the life-giving seeds that have been planted by way of others' words to take root and flourish in your own life; to the end that you no longer have to depend upon him, her, or them to speak hope for you. Rather, you can now speak hope to and for yourself.

Thoroughly convicted was I when I learned that the words coming out my mouth aided in perpetuating the defeat I was experiencing. Elated, however, was I to discover that when my language changed so did my circumstance.

CHAPTER FOUR

You Must Refuse to Compromise

"Anybody can say yes. But can you say no—and mean it."

Some time ago, somewhere among the many books that I have read I encountered this interesting statement. It's a statement that I can honestly say initially left me a little befuddled. However, after wrestling with the statement for a bit, I finally got it. And the statement was this, *"The right thing to do and the hardest thing to do are always one in the same."*

After I read this statement I laid the book down, sat back, pondered what I had just read, and then asked myself if this was really a true statement. Back and forth I went in my thoughts challenging all seventeen words as they came together to form a statement that I imagine was designed to do just what it did for me: Challenge one's thinking.

Over and over I kept saying to myself, *"The right thing and the hardest thing are always one in the same. The right thing and the hardest thing are always one in the same."* Then, curiosity pushed me a step further to dissect and break down the statement. I said, *"Okay, the right thing. I get that. I get the right thing. Now, for the hardest thing; what is this piece actually about? The hardest thing. The hardest thing. The hardest thing...."* Immediately, I began reflecting upon some of the hardest things I have had to do, and I put them in context with the notion of the right thing to do.

At the tender age of fifteen, it was a hard thing to break up with my boyfriend who was beating the hell out of me, and it was the right thing. In the 11th grade, it was a hard thing to tell my mother that I was pregnant...and it was the right thing. Upon getting pregnant, it was a hard thing to leave those streets alone, and be the parent my son deserved...and it was the right thing. In my 30s, it was a hard thing to release myself from feeling like I had to please everybody at the expense of never pleasing myself...and it was the right thing. After the death of my daughter, it was a very hard thing to turn my life and my self-destructive ways over to the God who was trying to get my attention so that He might position me for greatness...and it was the right thing.

As a result of getting married at the tender age of 20, it was a hard thing to try to find myself and simultaneously do the work necessary to maintain my marriage for 11 years...and it was the right thing. It was an even harder thing to pack my sons up and walk away from the marriage when I realized that I could no longer handle the mental toll the fussing, and disrespect, and disregard was having on me and my sons...yet it too was the right thing.

When I hit rock bottom, it was also a very, very, very hard thing to consciously decide to get up every single day, see my situation for what it was, live with as well as own the extent to which I contributed to my situation being what it was, forgive myself, put a smile on my face, and walk in faith believing that my change wasn't just coming, it was imminently coming...yet this too was the absolute right thing.

One situation after another I made the connection. Detail by detail. Blow by blow. Incident by incident.

Decision by decision. And without fail I had to unequivocally agree with he or she who coined the statement, *"The right thing to do and the hardest thing to do are always one in the same."* In fact, the more I reflected upon the different situations that I listed above as well as others I did not list, I could not believe that I even had to grapple with the validity of the statement at all. For the truth of the statement bears itself out in relationships, friendships, courtrooms, boardrooms, and classrooms all over the world—daily.

After resolving the validity aspect of the statement, I then went on to have another conversation with myself, because now I was in a zone. I was obsessed with extracting everything that this statement had to teach me. And so the conversation with myself came down to this question: Because it is the case that it is harder to do the right thing than it is to do the wrong thing, how does one keep himself/herself committed to doing the right thing when choosing otherwise is always an option?

I sat and I sat and I sat with this question. Again, I immediately reflected upon my own life. I juxtaposed the times when I did what was right regardless of how hard it was against the times I chose to do wrong because it was easier or more convenient. What emerged out of this time of reflection was the word *compromise*. When I chose to do what was right, I essentially chose not to compromise. Conversely, when I chose to do what was wrong, I chose to compromise. There were no two ways about. This is not rocket science. For at the end of the day, it simply comes down to a matter of *to compromise or not to compromise.*

Think about it for a moment. Examine your own life and your own life's choices—if you will. When you stayed on course it probably was because you refused to compromise. And when you strayed off course it in all likelihood was because you chose *to* compromise. Think about it. Now, I'm not suggesting you put yourself on a guilty trip of any sort. It's not that serious. I am simply attempting to help you get to a place where all of your decisions can be responsible decisions.

I tell you, when you are between a rock and a hard place. When the odds seemingly are stacked against you. When your efforts to do the right thing are consistently met with pressure and discomfort, you begin to ask yourself, *"Why? Why should I put myself through this hell when I could very easily do this another way and not have to suffer like I'm suffering? Why am I crying, and going without, and just barely making ends meet when a simple phone call could put an end to all of this foolishness? Why shouldn't I succumb to instant gratification if it's going to turn things around quicker?"*

Because isn't that what most of us want anyway? Don't we want the quick fixes? In our most desperate, vulnerable place, wouldn't we prefer to cut out as many steps as we can and get from Point A to Point B hassle free? Come on, let's be honest.

Well, let me speak for Mischa. If you are anything like me, you have not always been who you are today. Like me, you have, bless God, come up from something. You have grown. You have been changed. You don't think like you used to think. (At least not most of the time.) You want to be great. You want to do great things. And most recently you have come to realize that greatness is far from an overnight accomplishment.

However, the person you used to be and the person I used to be in our former lives didn't know this bit of information. And quite frankly we didn't care to know this bit of information. Rather, the person you were in your past life and the person I was in my past life knew how to get things done overnight. By hook or by crook was our mantra. We knew who to call. We knew when to call. We knew what to do. We knew how to do it. We knew where to go to do it. We knew where to go to get it. Suffice to say, we knew some stuff. We knew some people. We had a plethora of viable options at our finger tips—reckless though they may have been.

But, you know what I have since learned about having too many options at your disposal. I have learned that the broader your options so too are your consequences. What this essentially means is for every option you believe you have, you also have to consider (that is if you're smart) the consequences which are intricately connected to those options.

Where this becomes even more complicated is every option, get this, every option potentially has at least one to five consequences associated with it. You talkin' about work. It the event you have no frame of reference for what I am talking about, take it from me, it is *work* to maneuver through a multiplicity of options and consequences while on your way to making a decision to do something you *know* you have no business doing from jump.

Not everyone will admit it, but it is absolutely tiring – albeit easy – to keep doing the wrong thing and having to pay the price by way of living with the consequences either during the act or after the act is over; consequences that in most instances are good for nothing more than compromising one's spiritual, mental, or psychological well being. Ask me how I know.

What then is the message or the lesson here? The message or lesson is this: Tough times can easily turn into tempting times if one is not careful. Because of the pressure; because of the confusion; because of the sleepless nights; because of the overwhelming sadness; because of the pain, we tend to vacillate between discombobulated, anxious, and desperate as we endure what we define as the tough seasons of our lives.

It is in this discombobulated, anxious, desperate place that we begin to think crazy, off the wall, ungodly thoughts. And for most of us these are thoughts we have never had or perhaps haven't had in decades, yet because of the heaviness of our situation we start reaching for solutions without any regard for how they will affect us long term. Why, because at that moment it is about the moment. It's not about the long term. The long term will take care of itself.

What we need in the moment; what we are focused on is *right now* relief. How we can get some sleep—right now. How we can stop the tears—right now. How we can stop pacing the floor—right now. How we can stop the bill collectors from calling—right now. How we can get our blood pressure back down—right now. How we can again know stableness of mind and regain our peace…right now.

You may not like what I am about to share, but like it or not it is the best I have to offer. The most efficient and healthy way to endure tough times is to do just that: endure. Through the tears; through the headaches; through the uncertainty; through folk talking about you; through one disappointment after another, you must make a commitment to not take any shortcuts. You must make a commitment to not take any bribes. You must make a commitment to not give up. And you must make a commitment to not sell yourself cheat, because in doing any of these things you run the risk of further compromising an already compromised situation.

I cannot tell you the things that went through my mind as I slept on that sofa in my office. I cannot tell you the things I thought about having done to that real estate broker for what he did. My God! I shudder to think of where I could potentially be had I acted on some of the things that came to my mind. I shudder to think of the mental turmoil I would be going through even today if I had acted upon what I thought...even if I never got caught.

But, thanks be to God for keeping me and for giving me a mind to not make some of the calls I thought to make. How grateful I am that I ended up, through it all, constraining my old nature and doing the right thing even though the right thing was the hardest thing. And trust me when I tell you it was HARD!

CHAPTER FIVE

You Must Know When to Ask for Help

"Help cometh to he who beckons it.
But for he who stays silent help looks silently on. "

If someone were to ask me, *"Mischa, what was the most difficult part of going through all that you went through?"* The answer without blinking or having to think twice would be twofold: Coming to the realization that I needed help. And then actually getting up enough nerve to ask for the help that I knew I needed. Big, big, big deal for me! I mean overwhelmingly a big deal. I cannot tell you how big a deal this was. In fact, in my most honest place, I can today share that my tough times may not have dragged out as long as they did had I asked for help sooner.

Although I knew that I had a host of people that loved me and would do virtually anything in their power to get my life back to a place of normalcy, something in me would not allow myself to pick up the phone and say those four words that most of the world thinks is a display of weakness when in all actuality they are a display strength. And the four words are: *I Need Your Help.*

Only if you have ever had to ask for help can you relate to the knot that forms in one's stomach and the lump that forms in one's throat as a result of having to utter these words. It's something. It's really something. Some might say they are only words so what's the big deal. And, again, being perfectly honest, I once thought this way as well. In fact, being in the human service field for the past 19 years has given me my fair share of experiences with telling people how we all need someone at some point in our lives to help us put life in perspective.

I have been quick to impress upon persons that the word help is not a dirty word. Yet when the tables were turned; when Mischa now had to put herself in the place of the hundreds of people she once served, all of a sudden asking for help was not as easy as it sounded.

Picture having been homeless for a minute; staying from one person's house to another. Wanting so desperately to have a place of your own to call home, because that is what you have been accustomed to all of your life. It has now been four months that you've been displaced, and though you are most grateful for the hospitality, sleeping in other peoples' beds is quickly wearing on you. You know that you have no money. You are clear that you have no job. You are very much connected to the fact that you have no transportation. So, in a real way, if something does come along in the form of housing accommodations, you, by virtue of the dynamics that are your current reality, are somewhat limited where taking possession of a home to call your own is concerned.

Now picture getting a call from someone informing you that they think they've found you a place. The landlord, who is friend to the person calling you, wants you to come see the place and has already said if you like the place once you've seen it you are welcome to it. Your first emotion is excitement; excitement because you may finally be able to ditch the duffle bag; excitement because you may finally be able to turn the key to the door that you will call home; excitement because you and your son may once again live under the same roof, and excitement because, hell, you get to feel like a normal human being again. (In the event you have never experienced it, being displaced, without question, causes one to feel less than... in every sense of the word.)

But then reality sets in. The facts begin to line up before you. And before you know it your excitement is arrested by the next emotion: sadness. You're sad because with the natural eye you see no way that you can take advantage of this potentially golden opportunity. You're sad because the more you consider the facts that are before you, there seemingly are more reasons why you cannot consider the house than there are possibilities that you can make it work. You're also sad because this just doesn't seem fair on any level. Why would God even allow such an opportunity to come your way when He knows full well the reality of your situation?

This is not just *a* story. This was Mischa's story. This was Mischa's reality. This was my set of circumstance, and it was that last question in the paragraph above this paragraph that sealed the deal for me: *Why would God even allow such an opportunity to come my way when He knew full well the reality of my situation?* In my natural mind this was insulting. I was truly offended by the hint of a thought that God appeared to be working against me. I wanted to know what that was about. I wondered why He would do such a thing being the *just* God that He is.

However, in my spiritual mind I was led to pray. I was led to look through the lens of faith. And as I looked through the lens of faith I began to see the favor of God at work in my life on previous occasions. I saw how He made a way, literally, out of no way. I saw the days when He placed in my space things I could not begin to afford. I saw how He sent money out of no where when I had not a dime to my name. Through one vision after another, Spirit placed before me those times when I thought God wouldn't, and He did; times when I thought God had forgotten about me, but He hadn't.

Now equipped with the reminder of a smorgasbord of other victories which invariably ushered in a renewed sense of hope, I began to speak words of encouragement and promise to myself, *"Okay Mischa, you know what God has done. You know that in Him there is no failure. You also know that if He brought the opportunity of a home to you He has a plan for you to possess the home. This is the God you know. Now act like you know and walk in faith. Go see the house and if you like it tell the landlord that you want it. Don't waver. Don't fret. Don't focus on the tangibles that you don't have, rather focus on your God and His sovereignty. Believe in the power of belief and go get what God has purposed for you. The hard part is over. You've been in the valley, now its time to climb your way to the mountaintop. Restoration is here and you have to be to a willing participant in your restoration process."*

That being said, it was indeed time to roll up my sleeves, put my faith in action, and get my life back. *"But how? How was I to begin? What was I to do first?"* I asked myself. *"The house; go see the house. I need to get to this house that is being made available to me. Call somebody, Mischa. Find a ride. Ask to use someone's car. Ask someone to take you. Just get to see the house."*

Well, without a dime in my pocket for gas or money to use as a security deposit on the house, I called to ask if I could borrow my buddy Maurice's car. Without pausing Maurice told me to come and get the keys. I got the keys and in route to the house I began to pray out loud. I began to just thank God and bless Him for what I knew was going to be my new home. I began to regurgitate the words of His promise to me when I was at Lisa's house and I got excited that change was here. Just the ride to the house felt reassuring. The anticipation that welled up in my spirit was overwhelming.

After I arrived at the house I sat in the car for a moment to collect myself. When I looked up I saw that the landlord was standing on the porch waiting for me. As I got out of the car I started to look around at the block; at the neighborhood; at the homes and I thought to myself, *"I can live here. It's Westside, but I can live here."* The landlord and I am began to proceed into the house and no soon as he opened the door I was done. There was the same feeling I had when I purchased my first home. It was almost a deja vu moment.

Without walking more than ten feet into the house, the landlord said, *"So what do you think so far?"* I said, *"I like it. I want it."* He said, *"Well, don't you want to see the rest of the house?"* To him I responded, *"I don't have to but we can go look if you want to."* I just knew this was the house for me. I felt at home immediately. The warmth of the house. The character of the house. The immaculate condition of the house; the house just felt right in every way.

As we walked throughout the house, I could imagine me and my son doing what we do and being who we are. I could imagine my son putting his interior designer skills to work. I could imagine being at peace, getting settled in, and being real happy about the new place I would call home.

When the landlord and I were done walking through the house, I told him that I definitely wanted the house. I told him not to show the house to anyone else, because it was mine. He then instructed me to contact his wife about the rent and move-in details the following day.

Well, as I drove back across town those relentless monkey twins called fear and lack tried to climb back on my back. They tried to challenge me on the resources I didn't have to afford the house. The transportation I didn't have to get back and forth across town. The furniture I didn't have to put in the house, etc. But guess who wasn't going there? As I had told myself earlier, the goal was to focus on what I had, not on what I didn't have.

It was then that I began to talk to God. I told Him about my desire to have the house. I told Him that I wanted the house. I told Him that I was not going to look at any other places. Rather, I was going to trust Him for this place. Although I do not ascribe to the "name it, claim it" philosophy that is perpetrated in such a haphazard way in many of our churches across the country, I walked in belief with authority that the second house from the corner on Harlem Avenue belonged to Mischa P. Green. I didn't know how much the rent was. I didn't know if I had to pay first month's rent and security deposit immediately. I didn't know if they would do a formal credit check. I didn't know if they would ask for two pay stubs. All I did know was that I wanted this house.

Finally, I asked God to show me what to do next. For it is now August 1st, the new job I was supposed to begin wasn't scheduled to start until August 14th, and then we are not talking about getting a first pay check until two weeks or so thereafter. So I'm essentially looking at the end of the month before anything that looks like income will be coming in. Now . . . park right here for a minute.

The next day comes, I call the other landlord (they are a husband/wife team), I share with her that I absolutely love the house and want to move in as soon as possible; more like yesterday. I went out on a limb, told her that I was dealing with some unstable living arrangements, and as a result I really wanted to get settled into something right away. To this she replied, *"Great Mischa! You are welcome to the house. We'd love to have you and your son as our neighbors. My girlfriend told me that you are a special person. And it would be my pleasure to rent to you."*

She then went on to share that she and her husband ideally wanted to do a couple of things to the house before I occupied it, but if I were comfortable with moving in while they worked around us to get those things done she was okay with that too.

Without question, I was adamant about the sense of urgency with which I was operating from. Last but not least, the landlady told me how much the rent was. She said, *"We don't have to do a credit check or anything because you came so highly recommended."* (Look at God!) She went on to say, *"Just bring the rent when we get together to sign the lease agreement."*

Well, a couple of days came and went and the landlady and I were hitting and missing on a date to get together. It's now like August 5th, I do not want to stay another night at anyone else's house, and I am slowly but surely losing patience with all of the back and forth.

Finally, I called the landlady, put my pride to the side, and simply stated that I needed this to happen ASAP. She explained to me that she had forgotten about us getting together the other day and went on out of town for her husband's birthday. However, (hear this) out of fairness to me since she had dropped the ball, she instructed her sister to go to her house, get the key to the rental property, set up a time to meet me so that I could get the key from her sister, and help myself to moving in—while she and her husband where out of town for the next week . . . mind you.

Are you getting this? Without a signed lease agreement; without having paid the first month's rent or security deposit; without an inkling of how I was going to pay the first month's rent or security deposit, I was moving into a house that for all intents and purposes was technically out of my financial reach.

Thankful though I was for God's favor, it was not yet time to pull out the confetti and balloons as the uphill battle was not over; not by a long shot. Why, because, remember, I still was without any money thus no first month's rent. And I still had no way to get what few pieces of furniture I did have from one side of town to the other.

So where was the money going to come from? Do I rob a bank? Do I put my red dress on and swing around a pole on somebody's stage? Do I hit some of my old hustler buddy's up? OR, do I continue to trust God, refuse to compromise, and remember to operate from the premise that the hard thing to do and the right thing to do are always one in the same.

I am happy to report that I went with the latter. I stood my ground. I thought and thought and thought and thought about my position (the money I didn't have that I needed before the landlady returned to town), and I told myself that I needed to think outside of the box. It could no longer be about pride. It could no longer be about what others were going to think of me. It could only be about doing what I needed to do to get what I needed to get.

It's called help, Mischa. Like it or not you are going to have to solicit the help of other folk. This you cannot do in and of yourself. Regardless of how used to handling things on your own you are, in this season of your life it is about doing what you've never done to get where you've gotta get.

Resigning myself to this reality, I called a good friend and colleague of mine whom I highly respected. I shared with him my situation and his words to me were, *"Mischa, you have for years done great work in this city. You have been a blessing to a lot of people. People care about you. People love you. And I believe that if you sent out an email to just a hand full of individuals, you would be overwhelmed by the outpouring of kindness and compassion.*"

I mulled over his words for about twenty four to forty eight hours. I prayed. I got on the computer. I crafted the email message. I saved it as a draft. I sat back with an array of emotions and feelings floating about in my being. I asked the Lord to give me the strength to hit SEND. I got back on the computer. Went back to the draft email, and did in fact hit SEND. There it went. My "Help" email was gone out into cyber space; making its way to the intended recipients. But what would they think upon reading it? What would be their thoughts about me as they read about my situation? How would they respond? And then, most important, how long would it take them to respond? Because time is of the essence.

Well . . . at the risk of soaking my keyboard with tears from just the thought of how overwhelming peoples' responses ended up being, I will tell you that that one email yielded over two thousand dollars in cash (which by the way was more than I needed for my first month's rent). The email also yielded groceries, furniture, gift cards, thinking of you cards, emails with words of inspiration, prayers, and most of all a genuine understanding that HELP – as I used to tell my clients – is absolutely not a dirty word.

When my friend and colleague suggested I send out an email. When he told me that there were folk in my town who loved me and cared about me, I really had no idea how much so. In a matter of two to five days I went from not having enough to having more than enough. What a God! What compassion! What kindness! There's a scripture in the Bible that declares, "You have not because you ask not." How true! How absolutely true! The power is in asking. Yet there's also something to be said about living a life that *when you or should you* get in a position where you need to ask for help, people won't bat an eye at giving you the help you need.

I could not and would not be where I am today, with the peace of mind that I currently have had I not reached out for help. How thankful I am to God for placing it upon the hearts of so many to be so kind at a time when I had so little. I truly thank God for giving me the courage and the strength to reveal the truth of my situation. I thank Him for those who did not for one minute think any less of me because of the predicament I found myself in. But just as important as all of these things, I am thankful for the opportunity to share what my experience taught me with you.

Believe me when I tell you that you do not have to endure your tough times alone. People will help you. People will come to your rescue. You simply have to get okay with asking for help, and then you have to know who to ask for help from. For it is very true that not everybody can handle everything. So I admonish you to be very prayerful and strategic about who you entrust your situation to.

CHAPTER SIX

You Must Take Ownership for Your Part in Creating an Environment that Invoked Tough Times

"No sense in saying someone else made you sick when you concocted the medicine and administered it yourself."

Growth is not for punks. I know that sounds a bit harsh, but that is just the whole, straight truth of the matter. In my own life as well as in the lives of those around me I have gotten to a point where I absolutely, unequivocally despise excuses. Excuses unnerve me. Excuses tick me off. Excuses vex my spirit. Excuses throw off my equilibrium. Actually, if heard enough excuses can really make me angry. Why? Well, show me a person with a bunch of excuses and I will show you a person who lacks substantive movement, consistent progression, and/or any true degree of purpose in their life. Again, ask me how I know . . . .

Some years ago when I was hell bent on simply existing. When I was determined to blame everybody else for what was not happening my in life. When I just flat out refused to listen to the voice of reason, primarily for fear that something somebody said might expose me for the coward I really was, my life was completely governed by excuses. I was *the* excuse queen. I actually did not think anybody could come up with an excuse quicker than I could; that is until I spent two years co-facilitating life skills and parenting classes for incarcerated women. (That's another book all by itself.)

In any event, when my life was hit with what I believed to be the most impacting season of chaos and confusion I had ever experienced, I saw that I had begun to revert back to the person I just described. I noticed that I had gone back to some of my old, non-productive ways of dealing when my back was against a wall.

Initially, I stayed in this cocoon hidden away from public analysis and scrutiny. I talked to no one. I kept everything inside. I played the victim. And I was angry at the world and most of the folk in it. Why, because I had convinced myself that folk were somehow responsible for life not going well for me. Don't ask me how? I had simply conjured up the notion that somewhere out in the Universe lived a group of people who didn't like me, didn't want me to be successful, and as a result they were behind the scenes constructing this awful plot to tear Mischa down. Again, as foolish as this may sound, this was my thinking, and I was sticking with this nonsense.

That is until one day I heard the words of my former therapist saying, *"Mischa, you have to take responsibility for your own life; what your life is; what your life is not, it's all your responsibility."* Although in the core of my being I knew this to be true. I was not trying to receive it, because to receive it meant that I had to do something. And doing something was just not on my agenda—at least not in that moment. Instead, I had given myself permission to wallow, and complain, and cry, and whine, and blame, and point the finger...just like I used to do.

I can recall getting the news about how much more work my Saab needed after having just put a whopping four thousand dollars into this car in the months before.

The mechanic told me that it would cost almost another two thousand dollars to replace the rusted frame around the bottom of the car, which was already twenty years old. Was it worth pouring another dollar into such an old car, especially considering I had already, in a two month span of time, replaced just about every major part in the car; from the transmission to the ignition to the muffler system to the water pump to brakes all the way around?

The more I entertained my options, the angrier I got. I only had the Saab two years. I did not want nor could I afford a car payment. And going back to the auction to purchase another vehicle that I did not know a lot about was of no consolation either. *"I have to get the Saab fixed because it's the most viable transportation option I have at the moment,"* is what I said to myself. *"But then if I get the frame fixed and something else goes wrong, what then? Two out of three mechanics advised against fixing the frame, however, they have transportation. So why should I listen to them, they aren't going to be in the rut that I will essentially be placed in without my own way of getting around,"* ends the thoughts going on in my head.

Yet this wasn't the only thing taking center stage where transportation issues where concerned. About 45 days before my car started to act up my youngest son's 1997 Cadillac Deville that he purchased just five months prior to was hit and totaled by a police car zooming through the city with no siren on. A week after the insurance company settled his claim he received a payoff check. About three weeks after receiving the payoff check he purchased another really nice car and in less than 24 hours he blacked out behind the wheel, struck a parked vehicle, and totaled his second car. You talking about a lot to digest and take it...in a very short period of time. Whew!

Now, like many of us I routinely had a zillion places I needed to be in a day. I was accustomed to getting dressed, going out the door, getting into my car, and going about my merry way. How quickly that changed. Three cars down in three months time with no resources. This now meant walking around the corner to get to my office from my sister's house where I had initially been staying after I lost my house. It meant my son having to catch the bus back and forth to work. It meant not having the flexibility I was used to when it came to going and coming as I pleased. It meant depending upon people to take me places, and waiting for them in some instances to pick me up.

In a real way, I felt so inadequate; so helpless; so torn, and so angry. I just could not wrap my mind around the fact that I was in this unnerving predicament of dependency where transportation was concerned. I then became even angrier as I dealt with the fact that once again I had made some irresponsible decisions that directly contributed to me being smack in the midst of this not so pleasant situation. Not the end of the world, but unpleasant nonetheless.

You know its one thing when we find ourselves in between a rock and a hard place because of what someone else did. But it is another thing to find ourselves in between a rock and a hard place because of what we did to ourselves; or did not do for that matter.

Without resorting to indulging in a pity party that wouldn't change anything, I thought about how I was famous for waiting until the last minute to get things fixed on my car, which always made bad matters worse; which also always meant more money.

I thought about how my buddy Rasul had told me to sell the Saab not long after I got it because it was too costly to repair once things started going wrong. He even knew someone that wanted to buy the car. But no, I liked my car.

I thought about how I told my youngest son that he didn't need to be out that late the nights of both of his accidents, and how I should have demanded that he come home instead of giving him a choice, particularly because both cars were in my name; which meant anything that involved the cars involved me.

Beyond the situations with the three cars, my thoughts led me to ponder how I mishandled money. How I was not a good steward over what God had blessed me with. How I spent when I should have been saving. How I should have told my sons no instead of allowing myself to be taken in by the single parent guilt trip too many of us take ourselves on.

I reflected upon the days when I just refused to open the mail and let it pile up because I was afraid of what the letter or the notice said. (For crying out loud, they were only words on a piece of paper. How much harm could they really do?!) Then there were the missed deadlines and excess penalties that came into play as a result of not addressing what was in the letters or notices that I refused to open.

I was better than this. I was stronger than this. I was smarter than this. I knew it. This is not how I had always done things. *"What was different? Why couldn't I bring myself to do what I knew? Why did I continuously permit myself time and time again to not do what I knew I should have been doing? What the hell was my problem? Why not be proactive rather than reactive?"* These were among the many questions I began to ask myself as I looked at my messed up situation and was forced to take ownership for the part I played in creating some of the mess.

Often times our first inclination is to look outside of ourselves for reasons why things aren't going well. Quick we are to point our finger at this person and person. Quick are we to bring up this thing and that thing when the truth of the matter is *we* (in many instances, all by ourselves) messed up. We procrastinated. We let fear get the best of us. We did just enough. We failed to yield to our spirit. We ignored the red flags. We flat out ignored God's warnings. We told the lie. We went where we had no business going. We did the favor when we knew it wasn't in our best interest or in the best interest of the person we were doing the favor for.

Then the backlash comes that we somehow hoped would not find its way to us. Then reality comes to smack us in the face in such a way that we couldn't ignore it if we wanted to. Then (if we are smart and serious about learning something) comes the time to get honest, grow the hell up, reassess how we do what we do, and seriously make some conscious, informed decisions about how we handle the business of our life.

It's not about the never ending list of lame excuses we make for ourselves. It's not about the plethora of justifiable explanations we try to take refuge in. It's not about what your parents didn't teach you. It's not about how terrible your upbringing was. It's not about the people you don't have on your side. It's not about the trials you have had to contend with even as an adult. It's not about how unfair you think life is. Or how hard you think God is being on you. It is not about any of these things.

Rather, it's about stepping up to the plate of life and handling your business with integrity, with confidence, and with the assurance that *you do* have the power and the ability to make sound decisions. Yes, you have to actually purpose – by way of your thoughts and actions – to make sound, responsible decisions...every time.

So what you messed up for the first twenty, thirty or forty years of your life. So what every time you told yourself in the past you were going to do better, you slipped again. Damn it, keep at it. Keep getting up everyday with a greater intention to do what's right. Keep asking God to purge your thoughts and make them pure. Keep purposing to do well. Keep purposing to do right. Keep purposing to make yourself proud of you. Keep purposing to life an honorable life. Keep purposing to make happiness your daily goal. Keep purposing to lay your head on your pillow every night with a clear conscious, and before you know it happiness and a clear conscious is what you will have.

What was the past is the past, therefore, you are only held hostage to your past to the extent you hold yourself hostage. Today is a new day and now is the time to do things differently. Why, because your life is your business. And nobody is going to do for you or keep doing for you what you can do for yourself. Any one of us who have lived for a while on this planet called Earth knows by now that as sure as the sun sets and rises, things will go wrong. Life will show up. The unexpected will happen. Tough times will come. Yet the charge that is ours is to be *refined* *in* the tough times rather than *defined by* the tough times. Certainly we may not be able to control ever aspect of when tough times may show up, or how intense the tough times may end up being. But what we can control for, however, is the things we do to invoke unnecessary appearances of times becoming tougher than they actually have to be.

I pray, therefore, that you make a vow today that this will be the start of a new season in your life where you absolutely refuse to be used against yourself. I also pray that you will join me in embracing a life that is full of hope, full of stability, and full of happiness. Because as I have found out, it is *all* ours for the having!

ABOUT THE AUTHOR

Mischa P. Green is a native Baltimorean and the Chief Creative Officer of Greatness Now! Mischa is also an author, inspirational speaker, mother, mentor, and one who is committed to seeing persons live quality, wholesome lives.

Ordering Information

Name: _____

Address: _____

_____

City, State, Zip: _____

_____

_____Copies @ $10.00 + S&H = _____

Please send check/money order in the amount of $10.00 plus $2.75 per book to: 2327 Harlem Avenue, Baltimore, Maryland 21216.

For more information about our company, Greatness Now!, our seminars, the book tour, products, and other publications visit us online at **www.greatnessnow.org**. Please also feel free to e-mail us your comments, feedback, and input at **greatnessnow@hotmail.com**.

Other Books by Mischa P. Green

Revolutionary Revelations

Wounded Voices Unwise Choices

Sacred: 100 Affirmations for Girls

*30 Things He Told Me But Can't Tell You
Because You Won't Listen*